Super Sam Saves the Day!

**Written and Illustrated
by Mr. ChickenBiscuits**

For
Liam, Aisley, Jovie, Levi, and Maksim

Super Sam Saves the Day!
Sam the Dog Book Series, Book 9
Written and Illustrated by Mr. ChickenBiscuits
Author website: mrchickenbiscuits.com

ISBN: 979-8462992278 (paperback)
ASIN: B09G3C7FC9 (Kindle eBook)

Publisher: Mr. ChickenBiscuits Enterprises. Murfreesboro, Tennessee, USA

Sam had another new business. This time, Sam was selling perfume. He gave each one a fancy French name.

A bee landed on one of the bottles. But the perfume smelled so bad, the bee flew away.

Sam was testing one of the smells when his friend Mook stopped by. "Another new business?" asked Mook.

"Yes, I'm selling fancy perfume. Try this one."

"I smell like I just got back from two weeks in the kennel! I *love* that smell!" said Mook.

Sam said, "I know, right? Now, smell this one."

Mook sprayed it all over himself. "Wow! I smell like a wet dog!"

Sam added, "And you don't even need to roll around in wet leaves."

"That's a time saver," agreed Mook.

Just then, Kati cat joined them. "Pew!!! Why do you dogs smell so bad?!"

"Sam has a new perfume business. Want to try some? You can smell like a skunk..."

"No, thank you," said Kati. "I don't want to smell like a skunk. Or a dog. Not even a clean one."

Sam whispered to Mook, "Cats are weird."

But Mook didn't answer. He ran away after a squirrel.

Mook chased the squirrel up a tree. And high up in that same tree, he found his friend Sneaker! "What happened, Sneaker? Why are you in a tree?"

"I was afraid of a bee. I climbed the tree to get away, but I didn't see their whole hive! Now I can't get back down."

Mook tried to rescue Sneaker by using stilts.
But he couldn't reach him.

Then Mook tried a ladder. But Sneaker was too afraid to crawl past the bees.

Mook got a bow and arrow to knock the beehive out of the tree. But that just made Sneaker more afraid.

"No, Mook, don't!" begged Sneaker.

Kati joined the dogs and asked if Sneaker
was okay. Mook explained what happened.
Sneaker was not okay.

Sneaker said, "I'm not afraid... I'm only a little afraid... I'm not *completely* afraid."

Sneaker was completely afraid.

Kati tried to lure the bees away with some honey. But they didn't move.

The bees began to buzz. That just scared
Sneaker even more.

"I'm not completely afraid," moaned Sneaker.

As they wondered how to get Sneaker down, Sam came along and greeted his friends. Then Sam asked, "Why is Sneaker in a tree?"

Kati cat told Sam the story: Sneaker was afraid of a bee. Then he climbed a tree to get away. But he didn't see the beehive.

"We tried to help him down, but nothing worked. He's afraid of the bees. He's stuck."

Sneaker repeated his claim: "I'm not afraid. I'm only a little afraid. I'm not *completely* afraid."

Everybody knew that Sneaker was completely afraid.

Sam thought about the problem. Then Sam had an idea!

Sam put on his Super Sam cape and his Super Sam goggles. And he picked up a perfume bottle. Then Sam asked Mook to help him with the next part of his plan...

Mook jumped on one end of a seesaw and launched Sam through the air!

Sam flew right over Sneaker. And as he went by, Sam sprayed Sneaker all over with skunk perfume!

Sam kept flying and finally landed safely in a
big pile of leaves.

Over in the tree, the bees could smell the skunk smell on Sneaker. Sneaker smelled so bad that all the bees flew away!

The danger was gone! Kati, Mook, and Sam helped Sneaker come down from the tree.

"You did it, Sam!" cried Kati.

"Super Sam saved the day!" shouted Mook.

Everyone was happy again. The dogs chewed some bones. But there was still one thing to do to those stinky dogs. Kati found a hose...

Click or scan to see what happens next!

https://mrchickenbiscuits.com/super_sam_extra

Please visit:
MrChickenBiscuits.com
and download your
FREE
Sam & Friends coloring pages
(plus mazes, puzzles, and lots more!)

Printed in Great Britain
by Amazon